THE FIRST HUNTER

THE FIRST HUNTER

Robert SWINDELLS

With illustrations by
SI CLARK

Barrington Stoke

For Martin and Sinead Kromer, without whose tireless work with the Federation of Children's Book Groups, countless young people might never have encountered a great number of brilliant books.

1046787

First published in 2009 in Great Britain by
Barrington Stoke Ltd
18 Walker Street, Edinburgh, EH3 7LP

www.barringtonstoke.co.uk

This edition first published in 2016

Text © 2009 Robert Swindells
Illustrations © 2016 Si Clark

A CIP catalogue record for this book is available from the British Library upon request

ISBN: 978-1-78112-601-1

Printed in China by Leo

Contents

Chapter 1
Prints in the Dew

My name is Tan. I snatch meat. I'm Tan the snatcher and I'm fast.

I have to be.

Our hide-out under the cliff is deep and dry. We sleep here, behind our fire. Dip works with me. He has the fire that scares off the cats. He scares them off their kills, so I can snatch the meat. I'm fast, but he's brave.

I'm the Snatcher.

And Dip is the Brand-man. The stick with the fire is a brand and Dip waves it to scare the big cats.

So that's Dip and me. Then there's Gak and Lom who carry the meat home and Sil and Mab who are the mothers. Dol is the Old One and there are four Little Ones. Last of all is Wid, the Fool. We live together in our shelter under the cliff.

Wid the Fool looks after the Little Ones so that Sil and Mab can hunt for mice and frogs, eggs and honey. Wid's head is full of feathers and fur, but he's my friend. Dol is Mother to us both.

It is morning. The grass is wet, but the sun is coming. I get up from under the cliff and look down to the grass-land. In the night we heard a lion kill an animal. Now the lion has the meat of that animal, his kill. He's watching it somewhere safe and secret. Maybe under a clump of trees. I can't see the kill, but my nose can smell it.

"Tan," Dip calls. He comes out from under the cliff and stretches. "Are you ready?"

I nod. "Ready and hungry, Dip. Is Gak awake?"

"He's coming now. Have you got your knife?"

"Of course." I show him the sharp blade of flint. "And you – have you got the brand?"

Dip stoops and pulls a stick from the fire. I can see its smoke. It's still hot. "Right here," Dip says, and holds the smoking stick up.

A Little One gets up and comes over, rubbing his eyes. His name is Bub. "Can I come with you, Tan? I'm fast and strong."

"Fast and strong!" I laugh. "You'll be a Brand-man *and* a Snatcher, Bub." I muss his hair. "But not today, eh? One more winter, then we'll see."

Bub goes grumbling back to the shelter as Gak comes out. The three of us start downhill, leaving our foot prints in the wet grass.

The grass is long and yellow, like the lion's mane. "There." I point. "In the tree-shadow," I whisper.

Dip nods. "I see him. I see his kill too, four steps to his left." The kill has stripes, like the shadow. "It's a zebra," Dip says.

Dip bends down and pulls up some long dry grass. Gak and I watch the lion, who is sleeping, full of meat. Dip winds the grass round and round the smoking stick.

"Ready?" he whispers.

I nod. Gak nods.

Dip puts his mouth near to the brand and blows. The stick glows. The grass crackles. Flames leap. Dip runs at the lion. He screams and waves the brand over his head. The lion wakes, lifts his head and snarls. His mane is like the flames. The lion stands, ready to charge, but then he sees the fire. He backs off, growling, and stands over his kill.

Dip is brave. He runs at the great cat. The stick is high over his head and ablaze with fire. The lion roars. This is the worst part. Sometimes a lion will charge the fire, kill the Brand-man with one slash of its terrible claws.

This lion turns, trots into the thorn bush and looks back at us. It wants its kill. Dip follows the lion to drive it a little further away. Now it's my turn. I run to the zebra, slash open its skin with my knife and cut deep.

"Quick!" warns Dip. "Soon he'll charge the flames."

I'm working as fast as I can. Zebra flesh is tough, stringy. The meat won't come away. Then Gak is beside me. He grips the hoof and pulls. He's strong. He tears the leg from the zebra's body, heaves it onto his back and trots away as if it's the leg of a mouse – not the heavy leg of a zebra.

"All clear, Dip!"

I leap up, run after Gak the Carrier. I know Dip will back off slowly. He'll keep on waving his brand until he's with us. And when the lion sees what's left of the kill, still under the trees, it will lose interest in Dip. If he's lucky. Brand-men need luck and courage. Dip has both.

Gak walks uphill like a man carrying nothing. The others have seen him coming, seen the meat, seen Dip and me and no lion. They dance in front of the cliff where we can see them. They're laughing and singing. We're all hungry, our mouths water as we think of the feast ahead.

This time, it's only the zebra that's died.

Chapter 2
Jackal Dance

The meat is on a spit over the fire. It smells good. We'll do the Lion Dance while it cooks, then eat till every belly is tight.

Gak is the lion, a sleeping lion. He wears a lion skin. Its head is on his head. The Little Ones sit near by. They are mice and birds and lizards. They whistle and wiggle their fingers. The lion does not wake.

Wid is the kill. He lies still with a zebra skin over him.

Lom and me and Sil and Mab are Brand-men and Snatchers. We creep towards the sleeping lion. Dol the Old One sings a soft sad song – a song of empty bellies.

We are near the lion now. The mice and birds and lizards have heard us, seen us. Their whistles grow louder, their fingers faster. They are waking the lion. Dol's song grows louder too – and now her song makes our hearts thump. We hold our breath.

The lion lifts his great head. Now is the time. *Now.* Sil and Mab, me and Lom, stop creeping, start running. We scream and flap our arms as we charge at the lion. Dol's song is loud and high now. She rocks herself, screeches out her song and clashes two stones together.

The lion is up and snarling. He shows teeth and claws, he guards his kill. The four of us run at him. The Little Ones squeal and bounce and wiggle. They're so excited they've forgotten to be mice and birds and lizards.

The lion turns and bounds away. We close round the kill, pull off the skin, pretend to cut meat off the zebra. Now Wid curls up in the middle of us and puts his arms round his head. He laughs. The Little Ones shove in and paw at Wid's body. Dol's song ends with a shout of joy.

The Lion Dance is over. We stand still as we pant and grin and smell the meat we've won for a second time.

We sit in a circle round the cooked meat to eat it. Everyone is there except Lom. He's taken his meat and his spear to the hill top. There are many dangerous animals, even in the daytime, and so someone must always keep watch.

Wid is next to me. "Poor zebra," he moans and he strokes his chunk of meat. "Poor zebra."

I look at him. "Dip won that meat for you, Wid, but I'll have it if you don't want it – you can have a frog or some roots." I hold out my hand.

"No!" He sways away from me, and holds the meat tight. Then he turns back to me and says, "Dip didn't win this meat. Lion won it. Us like jackals. We steal meat. Our dance is jackal dance. More better we lion, not jackal." He starts to cry.

The Little Ones nudge one another and giggle until I frown at them to stop. I put an arm round Wid.

"Dip made the lion run off, Wid. That was very brave. He won the meat for you."

"We all won it," Gak growls.

Ever since Wid's body grew up and his brain did not, most of the others have wanted to leave him behind, to be eaten by wolves or big cats. "Why should we face danger to get food for him?" they ask. "He's no use," they say. But

Dol and I won't let them leave Wid behind for wolves and cats to kill. We keep him safe.

It's lucky we've eaten well. Everyone hears Wid call us jackals but they're too sleepy and full to care what Wid the Fool says. He's got feathers and fur for brains, they think.

That night it's my turn to keep watch, feed the fire. The night is still, with a clear sky and a moon as fat as our bellies. The moon floods the grass-land with silver. I sit on a stone, my spear across my knees.

'Wid the Fool,' I think. Most of the time his talk is like the chatter of rooks. But not tonight. "More better we lion, not jackal," he said. He's right. But how can we get meat? We have no claws, no fangs, and we're weak and small. How can we be lions?

Soon a wind springs up. It lifts sparks from the fire and blows them at the moon, as it rolls on towards the dawn.

Chapter 3
Bear

In the daylight I can see scraps of meat on the ground. Roots and berries too. We gather it all into one pile. There's enough food for all of us, for today. No need to hunt or search. We can stay by the cliff and be safe.

This is what I think, after I've been on watch all night. My head is fuzzy – I should know that nowhere is safe.

I'm sleeping by the fire when Bub the Little One cries out. "Bear!" he shouts. "Bear, bear, bear!"

I lift my fuzzy head. Bub is jumping up and down on the stone I sat on last night.

"Shush, Bub," I snarl. "It's too early for your games."

Bub's mother, Mab, gets up. She looks where Bub is pointing, then at me. "It's no game, Tan. There's a bear – a big one – coming this way."

I jump up and grab my spear. Of all beasts, the bear is the most dangerous to us. We live in caves and by cliffs, and the bear does too. Sometimes, our home has been a bear's home before we came, and the bear comes back, attacks us and drives us away. Also, bears don't see very well. In the daytime they can't see our fires. So they aren't scared of us.

I think I know why this bear has come. He can smell last night's feast. His eyes may be dim, but he has a keen nose. Perhaps he has followed the smell all night.

We stand together at the top of the hill. We're all there, even Wid the Fool. We shout and scream at the top of our lungs. We bang stones together, beat the earth with sticks and wave our arms. Sometimes, if you make a lot of noise, the bear will turn away. He can't see what's making all the noise – he hears it and sees something move. 'Is it a monster?' he thinks.

It doesn't work this time. The bear stops and swings his huge head from side to side. He sniffs the wind. There's noise, but he can smell food, and the food wins. He drops his head and comes loping up towards us.

"Dol!" I shout. "Take the Little Ones to the top of the cliff. Wid, go with them. If the bear gets us, run. Don't stop, don't look back."

Now there are six of us. Six spears, one bear. That makes our chances sound good, but they're not. A bear's fur is too thick for flint points. Ram a spear into that fur and it will snap. Hurl the spear and it will bounce off.

There is only one place to hit the bear – the mouth. The bear's mouth must be open and you must hit hard and fast. The point must go in the mouth before the beast can close its teeth and snap the spear. You have to hurl yourself forward to make all the force you need. And if your strike fails, the bear's great arms will pull you in and you'll die.

The six of us stand with our spears pointed at the beast. We'll have to fool him – that way he won't know which of us to charge first. We fan out, we dance on our toes and jab at him as he comes close. Soon there's blood on the bear's nose.

The bear gets angry. He rears up on his back legs. He's taller than Lom, and Lom is tall. He roars and roars and slashes at our spears with his long claws like hooks. We take turns to skip at him, jab him and skip back. The

blood mixes with the foam around his mouth and turns it pink. We hope the bear will give up, but he doesn't. He's hungry for meat, and he wants us dead.

All of a sudden, it happens.

Dip skips too close, stays too long. A great paw lashes out at him and cuts open his body from neck to hip. Dip cries out and falls, leaving his spear in the bear's jaws. The bear roars and bats at the spear with its huge paws. Pink foam flies from its open mouth.

Mab sees her chance. With a shout she dives at the bear and drives her spear deep into its mouth. The bear hurls Mab to the ground. She rolls away and the bear comes down on all fours again. It's shaking its head in panic to try to get rid of the two spears.

At last the bear turns and shambles away down the slope, the spears sticking out of its

mouth like tusks. They catch on bushes and
rocks as the bear moves off.

Dol and the others have seen our victory.
They come down with shouts and whoops of joy.
The shouting dies away when they see Dip lying
on the ground. Gak and Lom carry him back
to our shelter under the cliff. They put him to
lie on furs. Dol brings plants to rub where his
chest is ripped open. Sometimes a man will
survive a bear attack.

Sometimes.

Chapter 4
Until We Meet Again

Dip lies close to the fire. We feed the fire to keep it bright and strong. We pack his cuts with herbs, but at night the darkness gets into Dip. It leaves its stinking blackness in his cuts. Dip is brave, but that's not enough. You can't run at the blackness with a brand. Nothing will drive it away. The blackness melts Dip's flesh and turns it to maggots, which eat him.

Dip takes many days to die. His pain is great, but he never cries out. Dol is with him at the end.

One day, when we come back to the cliff with honey, eggs and roots, he is gone. Dol has laid the lion skin over him. The Little Ones sit silent for once. No one moves. Wid slumps near by. His moon-face is wet with tears.

We carry Dip away from our cliff to the leaving place. Dol sings. Her song tells how his spirit will follow the sun far to the west, where animals only eat grass and it is always day.

Fare well, Dip the Brand-man. Until we meet again.

*

"No Brand-man, no meat." Mab the Mother says this as we sit round the fire that night, thinking about our friend.

"Long ago," says Dol, "the people had no meat. They lived on small things – roots, mice, berries. We can do this too."

"We don't have to," pipes Bub the Little One.

Mab frowns at him. She is his mother. Little Ones do not speak out.

I smile at him. "You are brave enough to be our new Brand-man, Bub, but not big enough. I told you – one more winter."

The child slumps and stares into the flames. Mab looks at me. "I can fill Dip's place till Bub is grown."

"You, Mab?" I ask. A child does not speak out. A woman does not carry the brand.

She nods. "I drove away the bear, didn't I?"

I nod and look at Dol. "What d'you think, Old One?"

The old woman shrugs. "There was a Brand-woman when I was a Little One. Lidi was her name. She scared off many a lion." Dol smiles. "And a man or two, if I remember."

"What happened to her, Old One?" Bub asks.

Dol sighs. "Sabre-tooth tiger got her, Bub. We don't see sabre-tooths any more, and that's good. You had to be very brave to run at a sabre-tooth."

We all agree. When I snatch again, Mab will be Brand-woman.

Next day we don't look for meat. We are sad after Dip's death. We feel slow, not hungry.

Dol says, "I can't help you with this, but the bees can."

She means honey. Honey will make a slow man fast. Rotten honey will make a sad man laugh. Sil and Mab know where to go.

"There's a tree," says Mab. "A tall dead tree, in the middle of the forest. Bees make nests there – a new nest every spring. There are old nests full of rotten honey – enough for us all."

We all go except Dol. She can't walk that far. The Little Ones are excited. They want to run ahead, but we do not let them.

"There are lions," warns Lom, "and bears and snakes and leopards. Stay close."

The Little Ones walk near Lom and Gak, and look into the woods with big eyes.

We find the hollow tree. I look up. Near the top is a hole, and a cloud of bees. They would sting me to death, but Sil and Mab know what to do. Mab has a stick from the fire. She plucks handfuls of grass. Not dry grass, but damp green grass. She winds this round her stick, and blows on the end. No flame comes, only thick white smoke. Sil has put a rabbit-skin over her head. It has holes for her eyes and mouth. She goes up the tree, fast as a squirrel.

Mab goes after her. We stand underneath, looking up.

At the top, Mab waves the smoking stick in the cloud of bees. Sil sticks her arm into the hole. She must be getting stung, but she takes no notice. She feels about and breaks off lumps of honey-comb and drops them at our feet. The smoke is making the bees sleepy. Most of them don't attack Mab and Sil, but I'm glad I'm not up there.

Soon, there is a great pile of honey-comb on the ground. It shines, packed with honey. The two women climb down. Sil's arm is full of stings, but she doesn't care. We sit under the tree, fill our fists with honey and cram it into our mouths. The honey is so rotten, it makes us drunk. We laugh as Wid and the Little Ones fall down, shouting and giggling. Only Lom doesn't eat. He stands with his spear and keeps watch for danger.

When we've eaten all we can, we put what's left into a wolf skin for Lom and Dol. Then we weave our way back to the shelter. We haven't forgotten Dip, but we know he's happy, so we're happy for him.

Wise woman, old Dol.

Chapter 5
Wid's Game

A storm comes in the night. The sky throws down spears to stab us, and roars when they miss. Rain drums the earth and drops sheets of water so close to our shelter that Dol has to shift the fire. Wid is afraid of storms and crawls under my heap of skins. I hold him.

Day dawns misty. The sun is a pale, fuzzy ball. Our heads are fuzzy too, from the honey. Everyone is thirsty. We troop to the river, dunk our heads in the icy water and drink.

Now we're hungry. I look at Mab. "Pick your brand from the fire, Mab – it is time."

We set off downhill and leave Dol to tend the fire and Wid to watch the Little Ones. I am thinking two things – 'Will Mab protect me when I cut up the kill?' Then I think, 'Wid is right – we get our meat like jackals.' I don't like this second thought.

We walk out onto the plain. The sun is drying the ground and burning off the mist. We use our eyes, ears and noses to look for a big cat that made a kill in the storm.

After a long time Gak stops and holds up a hand. "A fresh kill lies close by," he whispers. He nods towards a stand of tall grass. "In there."

Mab bends down to pick grass for her brand. The sun has dried it just in time. We all look towards the tall grass.

Sil looks at Gak. "What sort of cat is it?" he says.

Gak shakes his head. "I can't tell, Sil. Even my nose can't work it out ..." he says, his voice soft.

"Is it a sabre-tooth?"

Gak shakes his head. "No sabre-tooths left," he murmurs. "I hope."

Mab stands up, blows on her brand. She must be afraid, but does not show it. "Ready, Tan?" she whispers.

I nod. "Ready." We can't see what we're hunting. That's not good, but sometimes it's how it is.

Mab fills her lungs, lets out a terrible screech and runs towards the long grass, with her brand high above her head. I'm at her heels, knife in hand.

Nothing happens. Could Gak have made a mistake? Maybe there isn't a cat here – and no kill?

Mab is three steps from the tall grass when there's a crackling sound. The grass sways and a leopard breaks cover and bounds away with a snarl of anger and fear. Mab crashes right into the stand of grass, jumps over the body of a deer and drives the angry cat further away. I crouch by the kill and slash through the skin and muscle to cut out the meat.

The leopard turns to us, growling. Mab runs at it, but it doesn't move. She stops, waves her brand, calls to me. "Hurry, Tan – she's coming!"

I rip the meat free as Mab walks backwards towards me again. She's trying not to stumble. Her brand has burned down so now there's only smoke. Lom seizes the meat and runs with it. Gak and Sil stand on both sides of Mab, spears ready. The cat comes, showing us its fangs. We might kill it between us, but it's so close, it will rip someone's belly out first.

Then Mab does something none of us has ever seen before. She blows on her brand and swishes it through the long dry grass. Flames leap and crackle. The cat stops and turns aside. The four of us push our way through the smoke, coughing. Once we're out of the smoke and fire we run. The leopard doesn't follow.

When we get back to the cliff, Wid grabs my arm. The Little Ones grin up at me, excited. It isn't the meat – it's something they've been doing while we were away.

"Come," Wid cries. "See our game."

I'm hot, tired and hungry. I don't want to see the game that Wid's made up for the Little Ones. He uses things he finds – stones, insects, bits of wood. Anything. It doesn't take much to keep the Little Ones happy.

But it's no use. Wid won't let me be. I have to go and see his game. I sigh and let him show me.

Wid has put some pale stones on the ground. And he's found a fishing stick. A fishing stick has a thin strip of hide tied to one end. You tie a bit of meat to the loose end of the strip and lower it into the river. Sometimes a fish will take the meat. If you're quick you can pull him out of the water before he sees what's going on and spits out the meat. You have to be very quick – better most times to eat the meat yourself!

For this new game, Wid has stretched the strip and tied the free end to the other end of the fishing stick – the end you'd hold if you were fishing. The strip lies tight against the stick now, so that nothing hangs down. Wid has made something new. He grins and I can see he's very proud of it.

"Very good, Wid," I tell him. "What's the game?"

"I do it, show you."

He's got a little stack of thin, straight sticks. He picks one up, puts its thick end to the middle of the strip of hide and stretches it. The fishing stick bends. He points the stick at the ring of stones and lets go of the hide. The stick flies a short way and falls into the ring. The Little Ones jump and shout.

Wid grins. "Bub is best," he says. "He can put three sticks in the ring."

"Good, Wid." I nod. "Good game."

He holds out the stick. "Tan do it. Better than Bub?"

I shake my head. "Not now, Wid. Bring the Little Ones to the fire. There's meat."

It *is* a good game. Maybe it's me who's the fool. Or maybe I'm just too tired and hungry to think.

Chapter 6
While We Sleep

The sun has gone west, to shine on Dip. We lie under the cliff, full of meat. We're happy. Mab is a brave Brand-woman – with her, we won't go hungry.

I sleep, but my spirit does not. It stands looking at Wid's ring of stones. In its hand is the thing Wid the Fool made from a fishing stick. "Tan do it," says Wid, but he isn't there. Such things can happen where spirits go at night. My spirit lifts the stick. It's not a fishing stick now. It's long and smooth, like a tall pole. Wid's sticks lie on the ground. My spirit picks one up and fits it to the strip of hide. It stretches and the tall pole bends. My spirit points the stick at the ring of stones and lets go. The stick flies, but it misses the ring. Wid and the Little Ones laugh, but they're not there.

The stick flies on till it hits a tree and bounces off. Dip is standing by the tree. He picks up the stick, smiles at my spirit. "If it had a point at its tip," he calls, "it wouldn't bounce off."

I wake then, and for a moment I think it's real. "Dip!" I cry. "You have come back."

"Hush!" hisses Dol, from her place by the fire. "You'll scare the Little Ones."

"Dip," I mutter. "He's back, he was talking to me."

Dol shakes her head. "His spirit was talking to your spirit, Tan. Go back to sleep."

We see all sorts of things when we sleep, but they melt in the morning like mist. But this one was in my head when I woke up, and it was still there as I washed in the river.

It is a day to collect small food. Roots, eggs, lizards.

I say, "There's something I must do here. Can you find food without me – for once?"

I watch Mab, Gak, Lom and Sil go off with baskets and spears. Wid is excited. He dances round me, saying, "The game, Tan. Play the game with us?"

"Later, Wid," I tell him. "First I must cut a tall pole."

The Fool leads the Little Ones to his ring of stones. I look among the trees till I find one with long, straight branches. I cut a branch and trim it, so it looks like the pole my spirit held in his hand last night. I take it to Dol.

"Have you got a strip of hide as long as this?" I ask.

She looks at the long, springy pole. "I have a strip of ox skin that's as long," she tells me. "I was keeping it to sew two big skins together to make a shelter from the wind." She frowns. "What do you want it for, Tan?"

I smile. "To make Wid's game better, I hope," I tell her.

Dol doesn't want to give up the hide just for a game but in the end she hands it to me.

I sit on a stone and cut a deep slot near each end of my pole. I tie the ends of the hide into both slots. Now it lies tight against the pole. When I hook my finger round the middle of the strip of hide and pull it away from the pole, the pole bends. My arm trembles from the power that's in that bend.

Wid and three of the Little Ones are laughing and shouting. They're playing their game. Bub isn't playing. He stands on a rock with his spear and keeps watch.

"What's Tan got?" Wid asks.

"This?" I look at what I have made. "This is a Wid-thing and a spirit-thing," I tell him. "Watch."

I take one of the long, straight sticks. I fit it to the strip of hide and I pull back with all my strength to bend the pole. When I let go, the stick flies over the ring, hits a tree and bounces off.

"Missed!" Wid shouts with a big happy grin.

"Missed!" the Little Ones cry, and they jump and jig up and down.

Bub calls from his rock. "If it had a point, it wouldn't bounce off."

I stare at him. "That's ... that's what Dip said." I feel cold, unreal. Is it me standing here, or my spirit? Am I still sleeping?

Bub stares back at me. "Dip? Did you say Dip?" he asks.

"Uh ... no." I shake my head. "No, not Dip. Listen, Bub, can you find me a sharp bit of flint? A little one. I want to make a spear-head, but smaller. I want to tie the flint to a stick. That way, it won't bounce off. It'll stick in the tree when I let it fly."

Chapter 7
Our Kill

It is many days later. A meat day. All of us are out on the grass-land – except Dol. Dip is here too – we can't see him but we feel he is close.

Gak can smell a lion. It lies with its kill under some trees. Mab looks at her empty hands. It feels wrong that she has no brand. Sil smiles at her. "This time we'll let the lion keep its kill, Mab. Today we'll have our own kill."

It's hard to keep the Little Ones and Wid still and silent. We need silence – the meat we're after is alive and on swift hooves. We step through grass as tall as we are. I lead, with the Wid-thing in my hand and a bundle of sharp sticks at my waist. They all have flint tips.

Gak hisses. I turn. "That way," he whispers, pointing. "Deer."

I nod and walk to where he is pointing. I pull out a stick. The others follow, Wid last.

I spot the deer. A small herd is grazing by some rocks but they watch all the time. They keep lifting their heads to sniff the air. But today the breeze is blowing the wrong way for them to smell us. I signal the others to stay, and I creep forward alone. Each time a deer lifts its head, I stop. Even my breathing stops. Slowly, slowly, I tip-toe closer.

The stick is in its place on the strip of hide. It has a flint point at one end, and a tuft of stiff feathers at the other. I draw back the strip, the Wid-thing bends and I feel its power. It will

hurl the stick from me to the deer – further than anyone could throw a spear.

I am close to the first deer. I daren't move, daren't breathe. I bend the Wid-thing as far as it will go, look along the stick to check it's pointed right and wait for the deer to lift its head.

It does, and it sees me. It tenses. In an instant it will whirl and flee. I let go. The stick flies out, flashes towards the deer and hits it with a thud. The point goes in. The deer bleats, snorts, shakes its head from side to side. Then it leaps away, my stick in its neck.

I turn. "Quick!" I cry. "It's hit, there's blood, it won't go far." I run after the fleeing herd, trying to follow the deer that's hurt. Mab and the others come behind, shouting and screaming.

The deer crashes through the high grass, smearing blood on stems. I can't see the deer but I can see grass rocking where it passes.

Gak catches up with me. "It's bleeding a lot," he pants. "It will grow weak."

We race on, and almost fall over the deer. It has stopped, with its legs splayed out and its sides pumping. A ribbon of blood stains its coat from neck to foreleg. The stick has snapped off, there's just a stump sticking out. The deer's mouth lolls open, pink foam glistens on its nose.

Everyone has caught up.

"Poor zebra," Wid croons.

The Little Ones laugh. "It's a deer," Bub whoops.

Wid nods. "Poor deer."

As we watch, the deer's front legs fold up. It falls forward and topples onto its side where it lies, shivering. I bend down fast and slit its throat. Then I spring up, push the Wid-thing at the sky and howl with joy. The others dance and whirl, grin and wave their spears.

It's only a deer, but it's our deer. Our kill.

Chapter 8
Lion Dance

Mab runs off to tell Dol what we've done. Lom puts the deer over his back and sets off.

I call Bub to me. "You won't be a Brand-man, Bub, or a Snatcher. Instead you'll learn to use this, and these." I hold out the Wid-thing and the sticks.

Bub grins. "Can I carry them home now, Tan?"

I grin too. "Why not?" He tucks the sticks under his arm and I hand him the weapon. It is as tall as he is. He sets off after Lom and the rest of us follow, laughing and singing.

As we walk uphill, we see Dol and Mab waiting. They smile to see Bub with the Wid-thing and the sticks. Lom has built up the fire and is cutting the meat.

"Time for the Lion Dance," Dol says, our lion skin over her arm. She loves to sing and clash the stones.

I shake my head. "No lion today, Dol. This is our kill."

"I know." She smiles. "Mab told me the story. We have made a new Lion Dance." She turns towards Wid. "Wid, come to me."

The Fool brings his wet, empty smile to the Old One.

"Put this on." She holds out the skin.

Wid gawps at it, shakes his head. "Wid not lion, Dol. Wid zebra. Poor zebra."

Dol shakes the skin. "Put it on, Wid."

The others see what Dol's doing. They come round.

"The lion skin," Gak growls, frowning at Dol. "On the Fool?"

"Yes," says Dol. "Today, Wid is the lion."

Gak shakes his head. "A fool in a lion skin is still a fool," he mutters.

Dol calls little Bub, takes the weapon from him and shows it to Gak. "What is this, Gak?"

"Tan calls it the Wid-thing," says Gak.

"Why does he call it that, Gak?"

"Because Wid made a little one, for a game."

"Wid made the first one, Gak."

"For a game, Old One. He didn't know ..."

Dol shakes her head. "No Gak, he didn't know. His head is full of fur and feathers. But when he looked at us he saw we were like jackals. He wanted us to be lions. This ..." She shakes the weapon. "This makes us into lions. From today we can kill like lions. We don't have to be like jackals and steal our meat."

So Wid the Fool puts on the lion skin. Its head is on his head. The Wid-thing is in his hand. The sticks are around his waist. The rest of us pretend to be the deer. The little ones are birds and mice and lizards. They squeak and wiggle their fingers. Dol sings a song of danger, but we are not afraid. We eat the grass. If the danger comes close, we can run. Nothing runs faster than a deer.

The danger is close. We look up. Time to run. Dol sings a swift song, full of leaping. We start to run. Nothing runs faster than a deer. But now Dol sings a new song, about how fast the stick flies through the air. It is faster, much faster than we are. We are hit. We run, bleeding. Our speed bleeds out of us. We fall. The danger is on us. Dol bleats and clashes the stones.

The Fool stands tall and lifts his arms to the sky. The lion's head is on his head, its snarl above his empty smile.

The dance is done. It is time to eat.

Our books are tested
for children and young people by
children and young people.

Thanks to everyone who consulted on
a manuscript for their time and effort in
helping us to make our books better
for our readers.